Contents

Cover illustration by Jan Lewis
Illustrations on pages 32-33 by Peter Stevenson

Published by Ladybird Books Ltd
80 Strand London WC2R ORL
A Penguin Company

6 8 10 9 7
© LADYBIRD BOOKS LTD MCMXCVII, MMI

Printed in Italy

Monkey business

written by Lorraine Horsley
illustrated by Jan Lewis

I can see a tiger.

4

Now I can see
an elephant.

I can see a snake.

Now I can see
a crocodile.

I can see a parrot.

Now I can see
a monkey…

Now the monkey can
see **me**!

I like chocolate

written by Shirley Jackson
illustrated by Annabel Spenceley

I like chocolate.

I like cheese.

I don't like yogurt
on my shoe.

I like bananas.

I like beans.

I don't like yogurt
on my jeans!

Fancy dress zoo

written by Marie Birkinshaw
illustrated by Alex de Wolf

We had a mouse in
the sitting room and

a rabbit in the hall.

We had a parrot in
the bedroom and

a monkey on
the wall.

We had an elephant
in the kitchen and

a tiger too.

We had a really good party...

a fancy dress zoo.

Our dog

written by Lorraine Horsley
illustrated by Ann Kronheimer

Our dog is too big.

Our dog is too quick.

Our dog is too small.

Our dog is just right!

New words introduced in this book

bananas   beans   bread   cheese

chocolate   stew   vegetable

yogurt   head   knees   shoe

don't, had, like, ou

Our dog

Boost confidence by reading the first sentence to your
child, and then encourage her to read the rest of the
story to you. You have already met 'too big' and 'too
small' in Book 3, *Sticker swaps*.

New words

These are the words that help to tell the stories and
rhymes in this book. Try looking
through the book together to find
some of the words again.
(Vocabulary used in the titles of the
stories and rhymes is not listed.)

Read with Ladybird

Read with Ladybird has been written to help you to help your child:

- to take the first steps in reading
- to improve early reading progress
- to gain confidence

Main Features

- **Several stories and rhymes in each book**

This means that there is not too much for you and your child to read in one go.

- **Rhyme and rhythm**

Read with Ladybird uses rhymes or stories with a rhythm to help your child to predict and memorise new words.

- **Gradual introduction and repetition of key words**

Read with Ladybird introduces and repeats the 100 most frequently used words in the English language.

- **Compatible with school reading schemes**

The key words that your child will learn are compatible with the word lists that are used in schools. This means that you can be confident that practising at home will support work done at school.

- **Information pullout**

Use this pullout to understand more about how you can use each story to help your child to learn to read.

But the most important feature of **Read with Ladybird** is for you and your child to have fun sharing the stories and rhymes with each other.

Learning to read with this book

Monkey business

This story of a girl's trip to a safari park introduces your child to reading animal words. Has your child ever been to a zoo or safari park? Which animal was her favourite?

I like chocolate

This light-hearted rhyme about the perils of opening a yogurt pot shows your child how one word, 'don't', can change the meaning of a sentence. This will help her to understand that reading every word in a sentence is important. You could use the food words in this story to write a shopping list for your child to copy.

Fancy dress zoo

This rhyming story helps to extend your child's memory by repeating animal and house words from *Monkey business* and earlier books in this series. Encourage your child to attempt to read the story for herself. Help her to notice the rhymes; it would also be useful to point out the similarities in the spelling of these words.

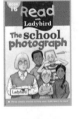